This edition produced for The Book People Ltd, Hall Wood Avenue,
Haydock, St Helens, WA11 9UL

First published in hardback in Great Britain by HarperCollins Publishers Ltd in 1995
First published in Picture Lions in 1999
3 5 7 9 10 8 6 4
ISBN: 0 00 762732 7

Picture Lions is an imprint of the Children's Division, part of HarperCollins Publishers Ltd

The HarperCollins website address is www.**fire**and**water**.com

Manufactured in China

THE FOX'S
HICCUPS

NICK BUTTERWORTH

TED SMART

The first stars were beginning to show in the sky as Percy the park keeper made his way home to his hut in the park.

He had been working hard all day and he was tired and hungry. Now he was looking forward to his supper and a good rest.

As Percy plodded on he saw his friend the fox coming up the path towards him. The fox was on his way home too.

"Good night," said Percy as they
passed each other.

"Good night, hic-Percy," answered
the fox.

The fox had hiccups.

The fox had been drinking some fizzy lemonade when a squirrel told him a funny joke about a parrot, a worm, and a cricket bat.

The fox exploded with laughter. It was then that he had learnt that it is not a good idea to laugh and drink at the same time. He had had hiccups all afternoon.

"I wonder if hic-Percy knows a good cure for hic-cups," the fox said to himself. "I th-hic I'll ask him," he said and with that he turned and followed after Percy.

When he got back to his hut, Percy remembered that he still had one or two jobs to do. First, he watered some plants.

"I'd better get my washing in too," said Percy. "Then, it's two boiled eggs for me and a pile of toast soldiers."

The fox hurried on. He wasn't afraid of the dark. He just liked the light better, that's all. But where was Percy?

He ran round the side of the hut, but instead of finding Percy, he found Percy's washing. Then, with a crash and a tumble which hurt his foot, he found a pile of flower pots.

"Oooowww-hic-ooww!" wailed the fox.

Percy was surprised by the crash.
He stuck his head round the corner.
But when Percy saw what had made the
crash, he quickly pulled it back again.

"It's . . . it's a ghost!" he gasped.

Percy had never met a ghost before. He felt he should introducc himself. But what should he say to a ghost?

Percy listened hard. He could hear the ghost still moaning and thumping about. Suddenly, there was another loud crash, then silence.

Percy was just beginning to wonder if perhaps the ghost had disappeared when there came another sound. A small sound. It was not the sort of sound that Percy expected to hear from a ghost.

"Hic . . . burp."

A smile spread over Percy's face.

P ercy poked his head round the corner again. This time, what he saw made him roar with laughter.

"Do you need any help, Mr Ghost?" said Percy, still laughing.

"Yes, please," came a muffled reply from inside the barrel. "Could you possibly turn me the right way up?"

Percy helped the fox back on to his feet.
"You gave me quite a shock," said
Percy.

"I gave myself one," said the fox.
"But it seems to have cured my hiccups!"

NICK BUTTERWORTH was born in North London in 1946 and grew up in a sweet shop in Essex. He now lives in Suffolk with his wife Annette and their two children, Ben and Amanda.

The inspiration for the Percy the Park Keeper books came from Nick Butterworth's many walks through the local park with the family dog, Jake. The stories have sold over two million copies and are loved by children all around the world. Their popularity has led to the making of a stunning animated television series, now available on video from HIT Entertainment plc.

Read all the stories about Percy and his animal friends. . .

then enjoy the Percy activity books.

And don't forget you can now see Percy on video too!